W9-BDE-379

AFRICA CALLING
nighttime · falling

Daniel Adlerman
illustrated by Kimberly M. Adlerman

St. Joseph
County
Public Library

JUN 1 4 1999

South Bend, IN

whispering coyote press

With special thanks to Amirah, Lou, Patrice,
and, of course, Dan
—K.A.

Published by Whispering Coyote Press
480 Newbury Street, Suite 104, Danvers, MA 01923
Copyright © 1996 by Daniel Adlerman
Illustrations copyright © 1996 by Kimberly M. Adlerman

All rights reserved including the right of reproduction
in whole or in part in any form.

Printed in Hong Kong by South China Printing Company(1988) Ltd.
10 9 8 7 6 5 4 3 2 1

Art direction by Patrice Sheridan
Book design and production by Our House
Text was set in 18-point Humanist 521 Bold

In illustrating this book, the artist first painted a base plate in watercolors. On top of that she applied
varying layers of painted figures in conjunction with leaves, dried flowers, rocks and stones, herbs and spices,
and twine. To create the dimensionality, objects were placed at different distances from the base plate.
Transparencies were then created from the original art, color separated, and reproduced in four color process.

Library of Congress Cataloging–in–Publication Data

Adlerman, Daniel, 1963—
Africa calling / written by Daniel Adlerman; illustrated by Kimberly M. Adlerman
p.   cm.
Summary : A girl imagines herself in Africa with lions, elephants, monkeys, rhinos, zebras, and other animals.
ISBN 1-879085-98-4 (hardcover)
[1. Animals—Fiction.   2. Africa—Fiction.   3. Imagination—Fiction.   4. Stories in rhyme.]
I. Adlerman, Kimberly M., ill.   II. Title.
PZ8.3.A2329Af   1996
[E]—dc20   96-11961
                                                                      CIP
                                                                      AC

j Pic. Bk.   CTR
Adlerman, Daniel
Africa calling

For Abby
—D.A.

For Bob and Wendy,
and for Savannah, Travis, and Trevor
—K.A.

Plains, jungle, desert, trees.
Mtumba, queen of all she sees.

hunting, prowling
lions growling

In the quiet solitude of dusk,
Elephant bares his mighty tusk.

mammoth romping
elephants stomping

As moonlight cloaks the desert land,
Viper slinks across the sand.

swiftly sliding
vipers gliding

Suspicious of each passing stranger,
Buffalo looks for signs of danger.

cautiously eyeing
buffalos spying

From the highest point of the tallest tree,

laughing, singing
monkeys swinging

In the deep, still calm of the river pool,
Hippo swims to keep so cool.

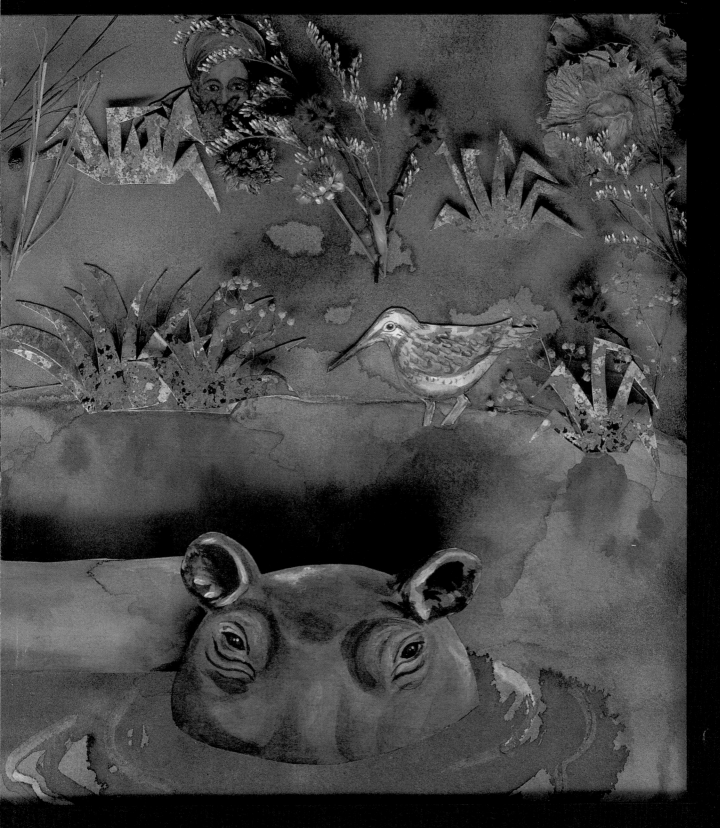

*splashing, spraying
hippos playing*

In shadows on the mountainside,
mysterious Zebra is trying to hide.

watchful, gazing
zebras grazing

Through marshes and grasslands rhinos roam,
this is the place they feel at home.

massive, stunning
rhinoceros running

Silently searching through night and day,
spotted Cheetah eyes her prey.

swiftly walking
cheetahs stalking

Slumbering through the darkest night,
I sleep protected till morning light.

Africa calling
nighttime falling

warmly beaming
peaceful dreaming

j Pic. Bk.   CTR
Adlerman, Daniel
Africa calling

WITHDRAWN
from St. Joseph County Public Library
XCESS X damaged
10/14/06